SECOND CHANCE AT CHRISTMAS

THE TRENGROUSE BALL

BOOK THREE

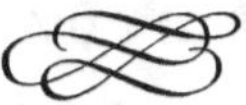

ELIZABETH LEYDIN

IMPROBABLE FICTIONS

THE TRENGROUSE BALL

The Trengrouse Ball…one magic night in a Cornish summer. Music, dancing, flirting and laughter. And deception, abduction, love and loss. New attractions, new hopes, and old flames rekindled. For some, a culmination. For others, a new beginning.

The Trengrouse Ball series follows the lives and loves of the Trengrouse family: eight grown children of the Earl of Trengrouse, each of whom is searching for the life they need; each battling their own fears but hoping for happy ever after.

After the Trengrouse Ball, their lives will never be the same again…

PART I
CORNWALL

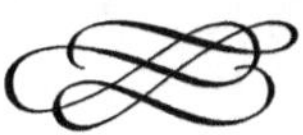

CHAPTER 1

It would have been pleasant to have lingered quietly over her return to Trengrouse Hall. But, as usual, Demelza Mandeville's two daughters chattered their way through it—past the gatehouse, where they waved enthusiastically to Edds as he pulled the gates extra wide for her carriage. And then down the long drive, flanked by young oaks (when had Papa planted those?), and up to the wide front steps where Mr Carveth had already opened the doors in readiness.

Her twins scrambled out of the carriage as soon as her footman had let down the steps, ignoring the, 'Girls, remember to act like young ladies!' from their governess, who held back as she should and allowed Melza to get down first. Nice girl, Sarah Lamb. A *treasure*.

The Hall was looking its summer best: the lawn lushly green, the scent of grass and roses and salt on the light sea breeze, every window shining in the afternoon sun. Melza wished she could feel more sentimental about it, but it was, in the end, just a very big house, and she had one of those herself. There was no sense of homecoming about it.

Then the family appeared, pouring out of the doorway.

Ives first, as usual, with his twin Melissa trailing after, Ives shouting, "Melza, by all that's holy!"

Then Locryn, the oldest, and his wife Elestryn, who looked paler than normal. She never did like the heat. Then Felix, bless him, natty as always, who swept first one twin and then the other up in a twirling embrace. Petroc limped out, still in uniform, crutches under his arms and an empty space where his left foot should be. Waterloo was called a victory, but it had cost Britain and her people dearly.

She forced herself to smile at him—at all of them—as the rest arrived. Mama and Papa, Kerenza who seemed little older than her girls, despite her eighteenth birthday ball being the occasion for the reunion, and finally, Endellion, a blond tower in the midst of the dark haired swarm.

And then, like a runaway carriage, Locryn's three careened around the corner of the house, grabbed the girls' hands, and pulled them away, with shouts of, "The stable cat's had kittens! Come and see!"

Good Lord, she had a big family! Noisy and chaotic. Kiss and hug and smile, one after the other, filled her up, finally, with a sense of coming home, especially when the breeze picked up, bringing with it the wonderful saltiness of the sea. Oh, she had missed that!

"Come in and have some tea," Elestryn said. Miss Lamb moved in the corner of Melza's sight to pick up a carpet bag, but Mr Carveth was before her, directing Bryok the footman to pick it up. Good lord, Bryok! When she left he'd been a lowly boots boy, and much shorter.

How long she'd been away. Since before the twins' conception, and they were six now.

Mama took her arm and they walked in the middle of the bunch into the Great Hall and through the double doors into the family drawing room, which looked out over the drive.

A large but informal room, with comfortable chairs and settees clustered around the fireplace, today filled with dried seagrasses and flowers.

Melissa sat next to her and looked her

over carefully. "You are lucky that black suits you," she said judiciously.

From someone else that would have been a shocking faux pas, but from Melissa… Demelza laughed. "Don't say that to any other widows, Lissa. It's not done."

Melissa nodded calmly. Talk went on around them, as it always had. Several conversations at once, with each of them alert for the sound of their own name, in case a sibling was promising something on their behalf or, in younger days, tattletelling on them.

As she thought that, Melza heard her daughters' names, Adelia and Grace. Papa talking to Felix.

"Yes," Felix said to him. "I call in on them whenever I go to London. We're fast friends."

So they were. Dear Felix. He was wonderful with the girls. She so wished he could have his own, but little chance of that.

Mr Carveth arrived with tea, flanked by two maids with heaped trays of cakes and biscuits. It looked too much, but eight Trengrouses plus parents and a spouse could dispose of a remarkable amount, Melza knew. The children would be given their tea in the kitchen; always so much fun.

She relaxed back into the settee and drank her tea, but she was still on edge. The interrogation would start any minute.

Sure enough, her parents sat nearby and examined her from head to foot.

"Well," her father said. "You need to eat more."

Everyone said that. Especially the Mandeville aunts, at the funeral.

"Leave her alone, Jory." Mama patted her arm. "She's old enough to decide how much to eat."

"Mandeville was solid," Papa said. "You're in good straits?" He meant financially, and financially she was in very good straits, thanks to a large dowry which had been Settled on her, and to John, her husband, who had left her a surprising amount of the unentailed property. For their daughters' future, no doubt.

"Yes, Papa. We're fine."

"And the new earl? He's treated you with respect?"

Melza almost laughed. As if that mouse of a man would do otherwise! "Well. He may not be the new earl, so he's treating me with a great *deal* of respect."

As sometimes happened, every sibling managed to hear that, and heads turned all over the room. Kerenza, her youngest sister, clapped, Felix's eyebrow went up, and Ives let out a whistle. Endellion, as John's executor, already knew.

"You're expecting!" Mama's face lit up.

Melza nodded, smiling, as she had to. But oh, how hard it was to smile.

"Early days," she said warningly. "John…" Her throat tightened, and it was hard to speak. "John didn't even know."

Her husband had been taken off by an ague, fast and unexpected, after a chill caught trout fishing when the weather had turned. Only four days later he was dead. Four days.

She'd been holding on to the news of her pregnancy until she'd passed the three months stage; it would have broken her heart to see John trying to bear up manfully under another disappointment. So he'd never known. She'd tried to tell him, on his death bed, but he had been delirious.

"I see," Mama said. She probably did, too. There wasn't much Mama didn't know about pregnancy and childbirth. And they'd discussed, only last year in London, the two miscarriages Melza had suffered through. Which was why she was *not* putting her heart into this pregnancy.

If she got past three months, then…then she could start to plan for the future. It was only another two weeks.

"So…you may put that prosy old Mandeville's nose out of joint, eh?" Papa looked positively delighted by the idea.

"Only if I come to term, and only if it's a boy."

"Well!" Papa said, bouncing to his feet.

"Something to hope for." He strode out of the room.

He never stayed anywhere long, and never explained where he was going, but they were all used to that, and fell back to eating and talking. Melza let it wash over her. This was home. Family voices, food she hadn't ordered, and nothing for her to do. Miss Lamb would look after the girls, and Mama would look after her, and there would be no decisions to make.

Heavenly.

"Guess who's home?" Ives grinned at Denzell Kelynack over the Kelynack billiard table.

"Everyone, I should think. Kerenza's ball was bound to bring the family in."

Den knew better than to seem curious. Ives was a good lad, but he was a care-for-nobody, and took positive delight in teasing his friends. Stalwart, though. A good man to have at your back. Den lined up his shot.

"Melza."

Pausing, as if to assess his line, Den drew in a breath. *Don't show anything.* He shot, and sank the red.

"How is she?" He tried for casual, but Ives' knowing look meant he hadn't succeeded. "Her husband is with her?"

Ives stood up straight at that. "You don't know? Oh yes—you were up in Scotland, but I would have thought your mother would have written you."

"Tell me what?"

"Mandeville's dead. Just over a month ago. An ague."

A month ago he'd been at a house party. Not in Scotland, but in Northumberland, at the Gunson estate. Long way to go, but Henry Gunson was a school friend, and they'd had some good fishing and quite a lot of whisky.

Mandeville dead. To cover his racing thoughts, he lined up another shot and took it, but missed.

Ives, against his habit, was silent as he

prepared for his own shot, and left Den to mull it over.

Melza was a widow.

A *new* widow. So definitely not someone he should be thinking about in *that* way. But how could he not?

He'd never loved anyone else.

They'd grown up together, had shared first dances and first kisses…so much to regret. Hope stirred in him, and something else, deeper down. Something like anger.

Would he have a second chance or would she headhunt a richer man than he, again? Did he even *want* a second chance?

"You'll have to play it gently," Ives said, startling him. "She looks as though she's been beaten down by Mandeville's death. And she's expecting."

Expecting!

That changed everything. If she had a boy, that would tie her to Mandeville's estates for life. A girl would set her free to live the life she wanted.

Of course, life on Mandeville's Gloucestershire estate might *be* the life she wanted. Certainly, last time he'd seen her, at Locryn's eldest's baptism, she'd looked like a happy woman.

Ives chuckled, and Den realised, flushing, that the younger man had seen straight through him.

"Always thought you two were well suited." Ives put some chalk on his cue tip, and shot again, cleanly sinking the next ball.

So had he. He rallied.

"What would you know about it, you stripling? You were barely out of swaddling clothes when she left."

"I saw enough." There it was, that odd maturity that Ives could occasionally show. It was what made their friendship possible, despite the eight year age difference. After his best friend Petroc, Ives and Demelza's brother, had gone into the Army, Den had needed a companion, and Petroc's younger brother who had always tagged on to their adventures had, it turned out, been the perfect choice.

"Well." Den shrugged. "Neither of us is who we were."

That was the God's honest truth. Also a lie. He was still the man who'd loved Lady Demelza Trengrouse.

He always would be, no matter how badly she'd betrayed him, or how stupid he'd been.

CHAPTER 2

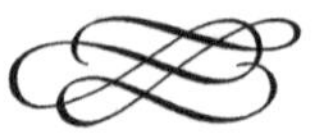

*H*er intention to do nothing lasted precisely one day.

Petroc was looking bad. Pale and sweating and clearly in pain. Demelza, as she always had, intervened.

"What do your doctors say?"

"They want me to sea bathe every day." He shrugged, turning away from her to look out the long windows of the library.

"Well, why don't you? The sea's not far away."

A hardness came over his expression, totally unlike the boy she'd grown up with. But she was the sister he'd always confided in. "I can't walk that far yet. Or ride. And the buggy—every bump hurts."

She put a sympathetic hand on his arm, and he let her. "I'll sort something out," she promised.

His mouth twisted in a rueful smile. "This may not be sortable."

But it would be. With a little thought and determination.

"Mama, your friend Abigail Marlowe—she's retired to Swain Cove, hasn't she, now she's the Dowager Countess? To that house her aunt left her? Semper House?"

Mama stopped going over her accounts and looked up, pen in hand. "What are you up to, Demelza?"

"Petroc needs to sea bathe every day, and he can't from here. But Semper House is quite near the sea. Near enough for him to walk."

Sighing, her mother reached for her correspondence notepaper. "I'd hoped to keep him home a little longer. You're right, however. I'll write to her."

So that was Petroc sorted. It was a month to the ball. He should be able to come back for that looking a little less like a ghost.

"Where is Melissa?" Demelza asked Bryok, the footman.

"In the small morning room, my lady."

Melissa really should be helping with the preparations for the ball. She'd always been adept at sliding out of group activities to go and read, aided and abetted by Ives. But she was an adult now – good Lord, she was *twenty*! Time for her to take on adult responsibilities.

There was a comfort in taking up the older sister mantle, but Melza deliberately didn't think about it. Perhaps she was filling her days with these old responsibilities because thinking about the future was…impossible. Until she knew if her baby would live

—until she knew if it were a boy or girl—the future was a fog of uncertainty.

Or perhaps it was just habit. As the Mandeville chatelaine, she'd run that house and the tenants—and, it had to be admitted, John—with cheerful efficiency. John had been… oh, he had been a lovely man, kind and intelligent, but disorganised! Such a procrastinator. And shocking at making decisions. It had given her pleasure to make his life easy, and he'd been touchingly grateful. She missed him so.

Melissa was in the small morning room, a cheerfully pale yellow place with a view of the oak grove. She wasn't alone, and she wasn't reading. Charles Goddard was with her—the Earl of Westholm, one of Petroc's friends.

They sat with heads together over a paper on the table.

"No," Melissa said with her normal definite tone. "It's not a subscript. Look, if we invert it…you see?" She said a word in what Demelza thought might have been Ancient

Greek. Melissa had been studying classics for years.

"Ah yes." Charles nodded. "Far more likely."

What on Earth were they doing? She cleared her throat and they looked up, startled. Charles smoothly took the paper from the table and slid it into his pocket, as if she'd demand to see it.

"That sounds interesting," she said.

"It is!" Melissa beamed up at her. "Charles always brings me the best puzzles."

"Puzzles? Shouldn't you be helping Mama with the preparations for the ball?"

Charles stood up with a slight halt in his step. Of course, he'd been wounded in the recent war. "A word with you, Lady Demelza?"

"When I was ten, you called me Demelza." She smiled to show she was joking.

"When we were that age, a lot was different." He led her into the passageway and checked quickly to make sure there was no one listening. Good Lord, he was acting like a spy! "Demelza…I would appreciate it if you allowed Melissa to keep working. She's translating a..an important document for me."

"From *Greek*? I didn't know you were an antiquarian."

A smile flashed across his face; really, he was quite handsome. But far too serious to be truly attractive.

"From the Greek, yes. I suppose someone in this family should know apart from Petroc…Melissa has been helping me for some years with code breaking."

He *was* a spy! For once, she was caught flat-footed, with nothing to say.

"I've been in His Majesty's service for quite a long time, in the Army and out of it." His voice was mild, but she could hear the warning underneath. "But I would prefer that not be widely known."

She recovered her voice. "Why tell me, then?"

"Because this code is crucial to the safe re-establishment of France as a stable country. I can't tell you more, but Melissa is vital part of the effort to avoid another war. And she *cannot* be frittering her time away on ball preparations."

"I understand. I'll make sure she isn't disturbed."

That smile flashed again. "Thank you. I'm in your debt."

As she walked back towards the Great Hall, envy pierced her. Lucky Melissa, to have something *important* to do. Something crucial, and vital, entrusted to her.

While the rest of the women frittered their time away on balls.

That had been unfair, and it rankled, but… if the baby was a girl, what would *she* be? The dowager of the Mandevilles, relegated to the Dower House, a mother but not a wife. Frittering her days away. At least if the baby was a boy she could continue to run Mandeville House, with all the skill required to organise the lives of upwards of fifty people. More, if you included the tenant farmers.

But she'd be tied there, for life.

For life, alone. Without John to talk her decisions over with. Without anyone to lean on. She shook her head and mentally slapped herself. Lean on indeed! When had she ever needed that? She was the one people leaned on, not the other way around.

As she reached the hallway, the side door opened and Ives came in, dripping wet. "I'll get you for this, just wait!" he said to someone behind him.

Denzell Kelynack came in.

Sir Denzell Kelynack now.

She should feel something. Something other than this cold sense that she was turning to stone.

She hadn't seen him since Michael's christening, but she'd been prepared then.

He stopped dead when he saw her and they just stared at each other for a long moment.

This was *nonsense!* She forced herself to move forward.

"Sir Denzell." She dropped a small curtsey, emphasising the formality of their relationship, and saw him wince. Good.

"Lady Demelza." He bowed, equally formal, and Ives, trudging damply up the stairs, made a rude sound.

"As if the two of you haven't known each other since you were both in leading strings," he called down, and then, wisely, disappeared towards his bedroom.

"A great deal has happened since then," she said, and coolly moved past Den and around into the other corridor, which led to the kitchens. She'd think of something she absolutely had to do there when she got there.

"Indeed." Was his voice critical? How *dare* he!

Fortified by righteous anger, she sailed down the hallway and didn't look back.

CHAPTER 3

He was going to be at dinner. Inevitably. Denzell and Katie, his sister, were such frequent visitors to the Hall that they were treated like cousins.

That was *not* why she chose her good black silk. There would be other guests there —Charles Goddard, for one, and probably others. Pappa always had some business acquaintance or other around.

Indeed, she noted five non-family guests when they sat down: Charles and Denzell, plus a Mr Gunson and a Mr Neville who were in deep discussion with her father about tin mines in France. Not the Henry Gunson who'd gone to school with her brother Petroc and Den; this must be his older brother.

And Mama had asked her twins' governess, Sarah Lamb, to sit down with them. Possibly to even up the numbers; there were far more gentlemen than ladies. Miss Lamb had the manners of a lady, even though she'd been brought up in an orphanage, so that was all right.

All through dinner she was conscious of Den, sitting across and down from her, as he talked to Melissa on one side and Kerenza on the other. Ridiculous to feel *anything*; and yet, she was aware of every movement he made, and the deep sound of his voice slid along her nerve endings.

She put her hand over her abdomen for comfort. That was her future. Denzell Kelynack was her past, and an unhappy, angry past at that. She turned her head away from him and spoke civilly to Mr Gunson about his plans to visit France.

.   .   .

DEN WAS thankful he'd been put between the two Trengrouse girls. He'd known them all their lives, and could keep up a conversation about sailing, which both of them loved, with no effort at all.

Melza was sitting there as cool as a cucumber. Not a sign that he had ever meant anything to her.

While *he* had to go home and tell his mother she was back. He kept up his company face, but internally he winced. That would not be a pleasant meeting.

Mel was so beautiful, though! Her girlhood behind her, her face was drawn in finer lines, the cheekbones more prominent, the complex hazel eyes framed becomingly by her dark brows. Her skin winter pale, though it was July. Goddammit. He dragged his eyes away from her and began to tell Kerenza about the prank he'd played on Ives that afternoon. Her laughter kept a smile on his face, thank God.

He didn't stay for port or for the musical performances and recitations which normally followed the men's returning to the drawing room. They were a talented lot, the Trengrouses, especially the girls, and usually he'd have done his bit, reciting some Shakespeare or Chaucer. In the past, he and Mel had done dialogues… he thrust down the memory of a scene from *Much Ado About Nothing,* where she'd played Beatrice to his Benedict, laughing and glorious in the candlelight. All in the past.

He wished Katie had been at dinner, but she'd stayed to keep Mother company.

He left early to catch them before bedtime. They were still taking tea when he came in. His mother broke off a spate of instruction to Katie about how best to sit down gracefully and smiled at him. She looked… all right. Not up in the boughs or fracheted. Well, he wouldn't have a better time. *Get over heavy ground as light as you can,* he thought.

"The Countess sends her regards," he

said, bending to kiss her cheek. "And Lady Demelza, too." Melza hadn't really, but that was only because he'd avoided her.

His mother went still. "Lady Demelza? She travelled so soon after her husband's death?"

So Mother had known about that? Odd she hadn't told him.

"Perhaps she was homesick," Katie said quickly. She put her hand on her mother's arm. "I'm sure she needed her mother at this dreadful time."

Good girl. He smiled at Katie with approbation.

"So, how is Lady Demelza?" His mother stirred her almost empty cup.

"I imagine she's fine. I didn't see much of her. I was out with Ives this afternoon."

His mother relaxed a little. "Well. I daresay she'll be going back to Mandeville House after Kerenza's birthday."

No doubt she would. He took a steadying breath. Much better if she *did* leave as soon as possible. That stare she'd given him this afternoon had been cold as a frozen Hell.

"I'm sure she will be. Could I join you for a cup?"

For a moment he thought they'd brushed through that pretty well, but his mother's hand on the teapot was clenched so tight that her knuckles were white.

Damn.

Melza went through the ordinary bed-time routine with her abigail without thinking.

"Thank you, Carter." Being a highly paid ladies' maid, Carter was referred to by her surname rather than her Christian name. A sign of respect. The servants called her Miss Carter, no doubt.

Carter left silently, taking the used linen and stockings with her. And there was the bed.

She had to get into it, at least. For the baby's sake, she had to sleep. But it looked so *big*. So empty. It wasn't usual for couples in the *ton* to sleep together, but she and John had always done so. His warmth had always been there in the night. Comforting, delightful.

Carter had turned back the covers. Melza made herself get in. Made herself sit in the middle of the bed, not on her side, or John's. There was a candle on the bedside table; she blew it out and watched the smoke rise in the moonlight which slid through the casement. Her tears seemed to rise with it, a thick, choking mess in her chest and throat.

She should lie down. Think of something else. Anything but John.

Den's face rose up in her mind's eye. No! Not him. Something *soothing*, not infuriating!

A light knock on her door startled her. "Come in."

Sarah Lamb opened the door, holding a lamp, and two little bodies ran in to the bedside, chanting, "Mama! Mama!"

"Miss Lamb?"

"It's all been a bit strange for them," Miss Lamb said apologetically. "I know you kissed them goodnight, but Adelia has been very sad, and so Grace is sad too. They're both missing Mr Mandeville. I thought seeing their mama might help."

Her poor fatherless kittens! She opened her arms wide, and the girls squealed and scrambled up onto the high bed.

"Thank you, Miss Lamb. They can sleep here with me tonight." She shook a finger at them. "And *only* for tonight!"

They chuckled and wormed in, one on each side, as Miss Lamb smiled at her and left.

"Goodnight, Mama!"

"Goodnight, my sweets."

Now she could sleep. She snuggled down, an arm around each warm, living body. Would it be very selfish of her to have them sleep here every night? Or would it be kind to all of them, including Miss Lamb?

As she drifted off, Den's face flashed across her mind, but this time it came with a whiff of long ago happiness.

CHAPTER 4

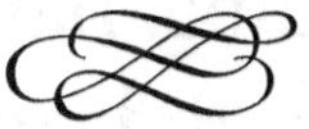

*D*enzell had done his duty this morning. Ridden over his estate with his reeve, talked to a tenant about drainage ditches for the back field, agreed on a price for a load of mackerel with a Swain Cove fisherman and, most importantly, checked on the progress of the hay. It looked good; it was a warm summer and the hay had been almost dry when it was cut, so they could bundle it into ricks with little chance of the spontaneous fires which could devastate a hay crop.

He authorised the hiring of day labourers

for the hayrick building, and then felt that he'd earned a ride over to Trengrouse Hall.

Demelza was avoiding him.

Or perhaps she just wanted time alone.

He left his gelding Barney with the stableboy, as he always did, and wandered up to the house through the gardens, hoping to see Melza "accidentally". He wasn't sure what his goal was. He was still so angry with her. *So* angry. Yet he couldn't stay away.

He just wanted to *understand*. How could she have thrown him away without a word? He needed to know.

She wasn't in the garden, but her daughters were, with Miss Lamb their governess and Felix Trengrouse. Felix was trying to teach them the basics of rounders, with much hilarity on all sides.

"How about I bowl?" he suggested, stripping off his hacking jacket.

"Excellent!" Felix said. "Grace, you field and Delly can bat." He positioned Delly carefully, bat in hand, her little face fierce with concentration. He knew that expression;

he'd seen it often enough on her mother's face.

The girls seemed identical in appearance, but not in temperament. Grace was quieter, more like Felix in nature, and one eyebrow was slightly higher than the other. He smiled encouragingly at Delly, and gently threw (you couldn't call it bowling) an easy pitch.

Delly slammed the bat into it and took off with a whoop. The ball hit him right in the stomach.

He fell backwards, exaggerating its strength, laughing and holding his belly. "I won't go so easy on you next time, miss!" he threatened.

"I won! I won!" Delly danced in victory, having made it back to the batter's mark.

"Not yet!" Grace said. "It's my turn now!"

"It doesn't quite work that way, does it, Miss Lamb?" he appealed to her with a smile. She shrugged, also smiling.

"I have no idea, I'm afraid. I've never played."

The simple statement, said without rancour, made him far too aware of his privilege, both as a baronet and as a man.

"Then you must now!" Felix said, but she laughed and waved him off.

"No, no. I'll just sit happily in the shade. *Someone* has to be clapping the good shots!"

They spent a hilarious hour with the girls batting and bowling by turns, with he and Felix coaching.

After that first hit, neither of the girls seemed to be shy with him, and they absolutely adored their uncle.

At a break for lemonade, brought out by Bryok, he mentioned it to Felix.

"Oh, we're such old friends! I visit them often; there's an ochre mine in their district Papa has taken shares in, and I'm up there monthly to give advice on machinery and so on."

That's right. Felix was a mining engineer. All the Trengrouse boys, except Locryn, had careers. Even Locryn managed the estate. Endellion ran their import/export business, Petroc had been in the Army, Ives…well, Ives was young yet, and had an estate in Norfolk, Kirwich House, which had come to him from his maternal uncle. Uncle Moxham. What a jolly man he had been! Always had a bag of boiled sweets in his pocket. They'd all loved Uncle Moxham.

He could be the Uncle Moxham to Melza's children. He'd tried to avoid the thought that he might have played with Melza and his own children like this. That the girls could have been his. Too much pain in that thought; but an uncle, that was fine.

"Mr...er..." Grace said, tugging on his sleeve.

"I'm officially Sir Denzell." He crouched down beside her. "But that's a bit of a mouthful. How about you call me Uncle Den?"

She cast a look up at Felix for permission, and he nodded.

"Uncle Den, can we go for a ride on your horse?"

He laughed. "No, lamb, that horse is much too big and energetic for you." Her face fell. "*But,* Katie's old pony is still around. I'll have my groom bring him over for you and Delly."

"That will be *excellent,*" Adelia said. "My cousin Jory has a pony too so we can both ride at the same time!"

Jory was Locryn's eldest. "Wouldn't Jamie's pony be a better size for you?" Jamie was eight to Jory's ten, and the twins were only six. He grinned to himself. How domestic this was; he knew this family so well, it felt as though he really *was* an uncle.

"No!" Adelia said. "Jamie's pony is old and slow. Jory's goes *fast,* fast as the wind!" She and Grace raced around the garden, pretending to be ponies racing as fast as the wind.

Felix laughed at the expression on his face.

"Don't worry. They're both good horse-women. Melza taught them. They have ponies of their own at home."

"That's a relief!"

Bryok appeared at his elbow. "The countess's compliments, Sir Denzell, and she'd be obliged if you would meet her in the conservatory."

That sounded ominous. Felix raised his eyebrows meaningfully.

"Yes, of course," Den said to Bryok. "I'll be right there."

"Word to the wise, Den," Felix said as he put on his coat. "Mama will be on at you to leave Demelza alone while she's so fresh from John's death."

What could he say?

"I'll reassure the countess." His voice was gruff, but he couldn't help that. Melza appearing in his life like this…of course he wanted to discuss the past with her.

Not, however, if it would cause her a moment of discomfort or worry.

And so he told the countess, when he found her among the palms and orange trees of the conservatory.

"I am glad to hear it," she said, speaking more formally than she'd ever done to him.

"The events of her first Season, and what happened then, are best left alone."

Did she think he had no right to reproach Demelza? She wasn't to know how close they'd been, but she must have known they were courting. Perhaps, in the heights of the nobility to which the Trengrouses belonged, marrying the very rich John Mandeville instead of him had been seen as an obvious choice.

"I daresay you're right."

"And the situation with your mother…"

"My mother is much recovered."

"Is she? Truly? I have seen no sign of it." She regarded him with pitying eyes. "I would be wary, Denzell, of allowing yourself to be so…responsible, for your mother's state of mind. It does her no good in the long run. And it does Katie no good at all." She gave him a dismissive nod. "We shall see you tomorrow night for the ball."

Well, that gave him his *congé*. He bowed and left, fuming.

She was so sure Demelza had made the right choice!

Had she? At this distance, he wasn't sure. Could she have lived with his mother without all hell breaking loose? Had *that* been the issue for Melza? Even if it had been, she should have written to him.

They needed to talk, no matter what the countess thought. He would go to the ball, and at some point afterwards he would visit for a frank discussion. Felix would tip him the wink when that was appropriate. Of course, it might not be until after she'd been delivered of this baby.

Which was months away. There had to be an opportunity before that.

CHAPTER 5

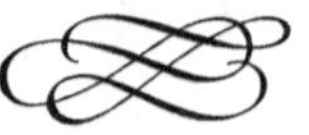

The small orchestra Papa had imported from Truro for the ball was quite good. Demelza sat on the top step of the stairs, Adelia on one side and Grace the other. The girls sat with their elbows on their knees, face cupped in hands, with identical looks of concentration on their faces.

They'd inherited her own love of music, and this was a high treat. The cotillion music came to a close, and a hum of conversation sprang up. Thank God her mourning state meant she didn't have to be down there, being polite! Kerenza's eighteenth birthday ball deserved better than that.

She couldn't bear talking to strangers at the moment, or even acquaintances. It was as though grief had stripped her of a layer of skin, so ordinary conversation prickled at her. But everything else she moved through in a fog, as though she were half-dead herself.

Not that she showed it. A lady didn't. Still, she was much better off up here with her girls than down there.

"Mama," Adelia said, too charmingly, "did you perhaps ask Mrs Lovell for some supper?"

"Yes, Mama." Grace nodded. "I am *gut-foundered!*"

Melza couldn't help but laugh. 'That is *not* a word a young lady should use!'

"I thought it might not be," Grace said complacently. "The stableboy said it."

"Hmm. You seem to have been running wild. Poor Miss Lamb!"

"Oh, we're always good for *her*," Adelia assured her. "We like Miss Lamb."

"But Mama, *is* there supper?"

"Yes, there's supper." A voice came from below them, on the landing of the stairs.

It was Den. Den, carrying a tray.

"Uncle Den!" The girls sprang up and went down to meet him. "Supper!"

Uncle Den? When did that start? Guiltily, Melza realised that she'd been far too lax in overseeing who the girls were spending time with; Miss Lamb wouldn't have known that this was a connection she didn't wish for. After all, Denzell ran tame at Trengrouse Hall, and always had.

She stood up, unsmiling.

Den came up, the girls following. He'd brought a tray filled to the edges with treats —far too many sweetmeats and delicacies, but…it *was* a special night, and the girls deserved some cosseting.

He smiled carefully at her. "I remembered the time your uncle Moxham brought us all supper at that Christmas ball. And I thought your little ones might like the same treat."

She remembered too. All the Trengrouse children and Denzell, together in the nursery, wishing they were downstairs, dancing. Katie and Kerenza had been tiny and had long fallen asleep. They'd all been playing Fox and Geese when Uncle Moxham had appeared, to be greeted by cries of joy and greedy little faces. What fun they'd had! Den had annexed the best cake, a cream and pastry confection, but he'd carefully split it with her and they had munched blissfully together, cream all over their faces. A spear of pain went through her at the thought of that happy little girl, who'd never known grief.

"That was kind of you." She kept her tone neutral, but knew she sounded cold. She tried again. "Come into the nursery."

"Yes, indeed. That's the place for midnight feasts!"

"But it's not midnight, Uncle Den."

"Not yet, Delly." He smiled down at

Adelia. He could tell them apart! That wasn't easy. Despite herself, she was interested. The fog of grief lifted a little.

They settled down around the nursery table, on chairs far too small for the adults. She wasn't hungry, as usual, but as usual she forced herself to eat for the baby's sake.

"Try these raspberries," he said. "First of the crop from the north field." *His* north field, that was, where the raspberries always came on late. He must have sent them over this morning.

The berries were sweet and full. A taste from the past, and the first time she'd felt hungry for days.

They shared so much. So many memories, so many shared experiences. It was silly to still be angry with him. And yet, a part of her was obstinate. He had betrayed her once, and could not be trusted now.

He and the girls were laughing and chatting like old friends. John had laughed and chatted with them this way too. The thought kicked her under her heart and made her breathless. She missed him so much.

"Are you all right, Mel?" Only Den had ever called her Mel.

"Yes. Yes, I'm fine. Just tired."

He touched her hand lightly, the touch curiously warm. She could feel the pressure of it even after he'd lifted his hand. How odd. It felt *real*; so few things were feeling real these days.

Staring into her eyes as though trying to read her soul, he opened his mouth, but before he could speak the door opened and Bryok came in.

"Beg pardon, Miss Melza, but Mr Denzell is wanted. Miss Katie's been taken poorly."

Den made a face. "Poor Kitten. Probably one of her headaches." He grinned at the girls. "Well, you two hellions take care of your mother while I take care of my sister."

He went out with a wave to the twins and a nod to her.

Just as well. She hadn't liked the look in

his eyes; it was the look of a man who wanted to get something off his chest.

She couldn't cope with anything like that right now.

DEN RAN down the stairs to the ladies' withdrawing-room, where Katie would be, frowning. Mel looked frail. She'd loved John Mandeville all right; her grief was obvious. But she was a lady, and held it in.

Curiously, it made him feel better about her. Far better to have been thrown over because she'd found love with someone else than to have been effectively jilted for a rich man's purse.

He could forgive her, if she'd loved John.

Now, to get his poor sister home before Mama tried to jockey her out of her headache. Any kind of illness terrified his mother so much…he wished devoutly that her fear didn't translate into bullocking poor Katie.

Particularly since Katie didn't have any idea why Mama acted like that; and never would, if he had anything to say about it.

CHAPTER 6

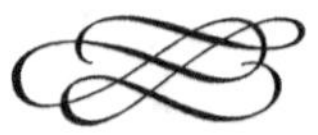

There was some kerfuffle going on about Kerenza having broken some precious piece of china after the ball last night, but Demelza could *not* take that seriously. The house, suddenly, felt too full of people, small and stuffy, despite the long open windows in the public rooms.

She needed a walk. She and John had walked every day. It had been a *quiet* marriage. No big ups and downs, no quarrels and reconciliations. They had just—lived. John hadn't been a demanding man, and she'd been happy to adjust herself to him, in the breakfast room as much as in the bed-room. Why not? He was a wonderful person. So considerate.

She took one of Melissa's hats from the cloakroom and walked out via the library, onto the terrace and across the West Lawn. There was a grove of elms by the stream...it would be cool there, and quiet, and she wouldn't have to talk to anyone.

As she reached the grove, she remembered, too late, that this was the last place she'd seen Denzell Kelynack before she'd gone to London. Where he'd sworn his love and devotion to her. Where he'd promised to follow her as soon as possible.

Where he'd lied.

It seemed like everything brought her to tears these days, even the memory of a long-ago betrayal. The tears burned her eyes, and she blotted them away with one of John's handkerchiefs. Her own were scraps of lace, too scanty for the crying she did nowadays.

She wouldn't let Den's perfidy stop her. This had been one of her favourite places on the estate, and she wasn't going to lose it because of a stupid memory. She found her favourite seat, on the low bough of an old willow near the stream, and relaxed back against the treetrunk in the welcome cool, listening to the murmur of the stream over the stones.

Peace and quiet. Just for a minute. Then she'd go back and make sure the girls were all right. As she sat, a hand over her abdomen, she felt it. The first tiny flutter as the baby quickened. Joy fountained up, filling her to the brim. The baby was all right! It was healthy!

There was still a little danger, but nothing like the worries of the early days of pregnancy. Once the twins had quickened, they had been robust and grown quickly. She was full of contentment and a great release of anxiety. The certainty drove the tears out of her and brought a smile to her face.

John would have been so happy.

.   .   .

WHAT A NIGHT! Den rode slowly down the long drive to Trengrouse Hall, rehearsing what to say about Ives and Katie. He should never have offered to break the news.

As he rounded the last bend but one, there was a woman walking across the West Lawn. Mel. He'd know her walk anywhere; and the figure was wearing black with a straw hat that didn't match. She'd probably grabbed one from the cloakroom.

He slowed. This was a good chance to talk to her. He'd said he wouldn't fret her, and if she seemed upset he'd leave immediately, but he had to know. To find out, once and for all, why she'd jilted him *without a word*. If she'd written… that would be different. But to wake up one day and find the notice of her engagement in the *Morning News*…it had thrown him badly. Especially then.

He just wanted to know *why*. Was that so ungentlemanly? Didn't she owe him that?

Before he could stop himself, he reined in Ive's mare and dismounted, tying her to one of the young oaks which lined the drive. Melza had disappeared under the elms. Probably headed for the old willow.

He followed her.

MELZA HAD FALLEN into a happy haze, grief at bay. Somehow it seemed perfectly reasonable when Den appeared through the trees. He was so much a part of this place. She smiled up at him and he checked, as though surprised.

"Mel?"

His tone brought her back to reality. Sitting up hastily, she adjusted her hat.

"Denzell."

Hesitating, he tapped his leg with his riding crop. No, that was Ives'; it had an ivory horse's head as the handle. She'd given it to him herself.

"What's happened? Is Ives all right?"

Den let out a bark of laughter. "Time will tell. The damn fool went and compromised Katie, and they're married."

"What!"

He told her the story.

"Poor Katie! And poor Ives. What a shocking thing, to be pushed into marriage without warning!" Den made a face at that.

"Better than to *not* be married, when you were expecting to be."

Well! At least he acknowledged that. That was something.

"I'm glad you realise that," she said.

Frowning, he sat across from her, on the stump of an elm Papa had cut down when she was only ten.

"What do you mean by that?" His tone was sharp. He had gall, talking to her like that.

"At least Katie won't have to wait, and wait, and wait for news of her-her beau's arrival, and then slowly realise he isn't coming!"

"What nonsense! At least Ives won't wake up one morning and find the announcement of *his* fiancée's engagement in the newspaper!"

She jumped to her feet.

"You'd thrown me over long before I met John!"

"I *never* threw you over!" Oh, how *dare* he!

"What would you call it? No letters, nothing at all, not even a message sent via Mama! I had to learn about your father's death from my brother Felix!"

He stood too, shock on his face.

WHAT WAS SHE TALKING ABOUT? She was so *angry*.

"I wrote to you!" he protested. "I wrote every week—sometimes two, three times a week!"

"You did not!"

"I did so!" The pain was clear in his voice, but he didn't care. How could she blame *him*? Then he recollected something. "I wrote care of your mother, so we couldn't be accused of a clandestine correspondence. I sent her a brief message with each one, telling her how Mama was, and enclosed a letter for you. But you *never* replied." They stared at each other for a long moment. Gradually, Mel relaxed, and sat back down.

"But...why would she?" Her voice was shaken. He knew how she felt; he was shaken himself. All this time, he'd thought London had turned Mel's head and she'd set her cap at the much richer John Mandeville. But if she'd never received his letters...Good God, she had no idea what had been going on!

And that was the answer to why.

"She wanted to sever the connection," he said slowly. He sat on the stump. "She—maybe she had reason, Mel."

"What possible reason could she have had?"

IF MAMA HAD DONE THIS—AND, somehow, she believed Den—she would have done it for a reason. But no excuse was good enough for the pain she'd been put through.

"You don't know why I didn't come to London." Yes! She'd been forgetting that, but

Den wouldn't have *had* to write if he'd come as he'd promised.

"I hope you have a good excuse. I waited–" Her voice cracked and she pressed her lips together. No, she wouldn't show *him* how much he'd hurt her.

His face was set hard, as if denying his own pain. The shadows of the elm leaves passed over his face, making him almost a stranger. He wasn't. This was Den; they had been able to talk about *anything*.

"What is it, Den? What happened?"

"Papa died. He had an apoplexy a few days after you left, and held on for another ten days…"

"I'm sorry." She had liked his father; a stolid, solid man who had always been kind.

"Yes. It was hard. But…Mama…"

He passed a hand over his face, and he was suddenly pale.

"You know Mama is…highly strung."

It wasn't a question. *Everyone* in the district knew how Lady Kelynack was prone to sudden anger and even more sudden vapours.

"When Papa fell sick, she… she couldn't accept it. Couldn't accept that he was dead. She was…"

HOW COULD HE DESCRIBE IT? Denzell shook his head at the memories. "She tried to…she kept saying that I would bring you to the Manor as my wife, and then there'd be no role for her, nothing for her to live for… She tried… we had to watch her, day and night."

The memories assaulted him. The hysterics, the moaning, the refusal to eat.

"Den…" Mel's voice was soft, compassionate. He pushed down a surge of self-pity. He had to make her understand.

"I had to keep Katie out of it. She came to stay at the Hall, with your governess and the younger children. But if I left the Manor, Mama became…" He paused, and then went on resolutely. She had to know the worst. "I came back once, just in time to stop her throwing herself out the window, sobbing that I'd abandoned her."

The responsibility that had settled on his shoulders at that moment…as well as the sudden burden of managing the estate and the house, with no support.

"We would have helped," Mel said gently.

"You'd gone to London. Anyone who could help was in Town for the Season. And I was desperate that the news not get out. For Katie's sake. What chances would she have had, if people thought her mother was–was mad? The servants were loyal, but once I told someone else… the only person I trusted was your mother."

Mel got up and came to him; placed a comforting hand on his shoulder.

"And she–"

"And she betrayed me. Betrayed *both* of us."

He looked up at her; she had tears on her face. For him? For Mama? For herself?

"Bad blood," he said bitterly. "That's what she would have thought to herself. Bad blood, and better if Demelza doesn't marry into that family."

Her hand clenched on his shoulder. "She let me believe that you'd just—dropped me."

"I find that very hard to forgive. She could at least have told you the truth."

Mel laughed shortly, moving back to her willow. "Oh, no! Mama would have known that I would have posted straight back here to you."

Their eyes met in a long gaze. A look which reshaped the past and let go of disappointment and heartache.

"I'm glad," he said simply. "I'm glad you didn't throw me over."

This time, her laugh was genuine. "I can say the same!"

He reached out a hand to her. "Friends, then?" At that moment, he wanted her friendship so badly. There had been a hole in his life since she'd left that nothing could fill.

"Friends," she agreed, putting her hand in his.

But as soon as they touched, he knew that friendship was the least he wanted from her.

THEY WALKED BACK to the Hall, Den leading Ives' mare. So many emotions churned in her, but the strongest was anger at her mother.

"Will you speak to your mother?" Den asked.

"No. There's no point. It's clear what she did and why she did it. It's all in the past."

It *wasn't*. It hurt. Hurt almost unbearably that the one person she'd trusted with her feelings about Den had ignored those and chosen to make decisions on her behalf. She would never do so for her own girls. She would *advise* them, yes, but she wouldn't lie to them and break their hearts.

She had to admit, though, that she'd probably advise them to avoid a family with this type of problem. Bad blood…

Thinking over what she knew of Lady Kelynack, though…

"Have you ever thought, Den, that your mother…exaggerated how she felt, to keep you there? She's never liked me, you know."

"Demelza! If you'd *seen* her…" He fell silent. "No. No. It was genuine grief, brought to a boiling point by her own temperament. She had relied on my father for so much… You're too hard on her."

"*I'm* a widow with children, grieving a man I loved. No matter how difficult it is, it's my duty to look after them."

"But they're children. I was a man."

"Katie wasn't."

"Katie had me."

Perhaps. Perhaps it was as simple as that. Still, just as Lady Kelynack had never liked her, Melza had never liked Den's mother. She was angry at both mothers.

It made her guilty that it came as relief to be angry rather than sorrowful. Along with the anger came a fugitive happiness. She had her old friend back; and, better, he had never betrayed her, never abandoned her, never lied to her.

That was worth a great deal. Better to let her anger go, and get on with living.

DEN RODE home in a brown study after the dust settled from Ives and Katie's marriage.

While relieved that Katie had settled fairly happily into Trengrouse Hall, he couldn't spare a thought for that. The fact that the Countess had scuttled his courtship of Mel had given him a leveller.

His dark resentment of Demelza had been…it had been a foundation of his life. A grim layer on which he'd built his adult self. Never trusting. Never daring to marry.

And how much of that was about Demelza, and how much about his mother?

Well, he'd been right to be untrusting—he'd just blamed the wrong Trengrouse woman. How *dare* the Countess?

And yet…he understood. If Katie had wanted to marry into a family with a history of…of instability…he would have tried to dissuade her. But he would also have explained why to her suitor. *That* was what he couldn't forgive; the Countess should have told him the truth. He would have understood—by God, the state he'd been in, he would have! He'd doubted his own sanity sometimes.

His mother...

He couldn't believe Mel was right when she suggested that Mother had, well, *exaggerated* was the kindest word he could think of. Surely not.

That night he'd come back to find her half out the window...how much of a coincidence was it that she'd tried to jump just as he walked through the door?

No. Surely not. The very thought made him sick to his guts. Impossible.

Surely?

CHAPTER 7

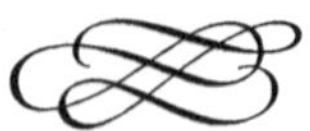

The more she thought it over, the less Demelza understood her mother's behaviour. After all, she hadn't raised any objections to Katie being part of the family. On the contrary, she'd welcomed Katie with open arms, clearly delighted with her being Ives' wife, although a bit bemused, as they all were.

Still, it had been years…perhaps her mother had realised that Lady Kelynack wasn't as unstable as she had thought.

She had to ask. She waited until they were together in the cabinet room, returning the precious pieces of display china, taken out for the ball, to their cupboards. The children were off pretending to hunt a baboon, of all things, and most of the ball guests had left. The house was quiet.

"Why did you not give me Den's letters?" she asked simply.

"Ah," her mother said. No sign of guilt. Just resignation. "I suppose it had to come out, now that you're on speaking terms."

"Yes."

They were so alike, she and her mother. Practical women. *Managing* females. Both of them the eldest girl in their families, used to taking responsibility for others.

Mama took a long breath in, and let it out. "I didn't think you'd be happy together. In that house. With that woman."

"There's a dower house. She could have gone to live there."

Putting a Sèvres vase into a low cupboard, her mother laughed shortly, then stood and gazed at her. "Do you honestly think Denzell Kelynack would have made his mother leave her home? When she was mad with grief? No, my girl. You were well out of that. I had my duty to you, and I did it."

And that explained why she didn't mind Katie. Katie had *left* Kelynack House by marrying Ives.

"John was a good man," Mama went on. "And you loved him. Didn't you?" Her voice, for the first time, was anxious.

"Yes." Melza slid a gold-rimmed fruit bowl onto the shelf. "I did. And I mourn him."

Her mother came over and laid a hand on Mel's sleeve, her face solemn.

"Be careful, Melza. That woman is still there. And Denzell Kelynack hasn't changed. He won't oust her for you. Not ever. And she'll do everything in her power to make sure of that."

Demelza pulled away. "Oh, for Heaven's sake, Mama! I've just buried one husband. I'm not looking for another."

"You understand why I did it?"

"I understand." She stared straight into

her mother's eyes. "I don't condone it. You were wrong to decide on how I should live my life. It's *my* life, and I had the right to choose my husband."

Rigid, Mama nodded and took a step back. "Perhaps that's true, although it's not a right I ever had. But I'll remind you of those words if your daughters ever want to marry unwisely."

Oh, the temptation to flounce out of the room as if she were still that young, untried woman! Demelza curtailed it, and took another bowl from the table, taking care not to leave fingerprints on the shiny gold inlay.

"I'll look forward to that," she said. She slid the bowl onto the cupboard shelf with a snap.

OVER DINNER, Den watched his mother. Katie's marriage had lifted some kind of burden from her; he hadn't understood how anxious she'd been about it until now, when she was happy and light-hearted as he'd rarely seen her.

"You don't mind too much about Katie and Ives?"

She made a face. "It's a crying shame! To have to throw herself away on a younger son – the *youngest* son, at that. I had such hopes for her Season! But he inherited that manor in Suffolk or somewhere odd. He's not a pauper. And she'll be safe with him."

That was odd. "Safe?"

"Oh yes. You can't put too much importance on a young woman being *safe* with her husband. Some men…" She shook her head, solemnly. He heard the echo of his grandmother's voice in her words. His mother's mother had been an anxious woman, starting at shadows, sure every sniffle was consumption, every shadow on the road a highwayman. If one were raised by a woman like that, one would naturally be anxious too. He *tried* to be understanding of Mama's flights, he honestly did.

His mother had gone on with her meal

with complete unconcern. Not for the first time, he wondered if she actually cared about Katie. So often in their childhood, Katie's needs had been ignored or pushed aside to favour him. He'd fought against it, but his father had shrugged. "It's natural for a mother to love a son more," he'd said. But was it natural for a mother to have little care for her daughter?

There was no doubting it: his mother was *odd*.

Odd was as good a word as any. Hard to believe she was as manipulative as Mel had implied, though.

"I daresay that the Countess will invite me to London for the Season," Mama said, in alt. "I won't even have to hire a London house!"

"But Katie doesn't need a Season now."

She fixed him with an admonitory eye. "She must still be introduced to the *ton*. And I will be there with her, as her chaperone."

"Mama, she doesn't need a chaperone any more. She's a married woman."

Fury flashed across her face so fast he thought he'd imagined it.

"She will need someone to teach her how to go on. That is a mother's duty, and I will perform it, no matter how much effort it costs me, or how little the gratitude she will show!"

Slapping her napkin down on the table, she rose and headed for the drawingroom. Thank God she was a stickler for the forms of etiquette. He had a few quiet moments to drink port before he had to join her.

He'd taken his duties for granted for so long, but all this marriage business, Mel coming back, the revelations…suddenly he was aware that the prospect of a night spent listening to Mama's plans for London was insupportable.

Well, Ives might be married, but their friends in Swain Cove were not. The butler came in with the port. Den pushed back from the table.

"Give my mother my regrets, but I've been called away."

Chegwin nodded, his face impassive, though his eyes were full of understanding.

Damn it. Servants knew everything.

He just couldn't stare at Mama tonight, knowing her instability had cost him Demelza. As the footman helped him on with his driving coat, that hit him in the gut. But for Mama…

But for Mama he might have been happy.

The thought sent him out into the night, thankful that the moon was only just past full, so he could ride into the darkness and leave it all behind him.

PART II
GLOUCESTERSHIRE

CHAPTER 8

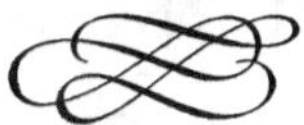

FIVE MONTHS LATER: DECEMBER, 1815

MANDEVILLE HOUSE

Surely having twins had been more uncomfortable than this? Demelza was doubtful. Her back had never been this bad. She eased forward on the sofa and Katie rushed to put a cushion behind her.

"Thank you."

Katie smiled and poured her another cup of tea. Better not to drink it. There was a retiring closet on this floor, but she'd already visited it twice this afternoon. So embarrassing.

"Is there anything else I can get you?"

"No, thank you." Katie was, apparently, intrigued by everything about pregnancy. Only natural in a young wife, wondering when her turn would come. Her solicitude was wearing Demelza to a frazzle. She was a lovely girl, but since the family had decided to descend on her for Christmas, her help wasn't needed. Her father had said that they all needed a change of scenery, but she knew they were there to help the twins, and her, over the grief of their first Christmas without John.

Mama sailed into the room, sliding her furs off into the waiting hands of Jonas the footman, who had conceived an intense hero-worship of her mother the minute he'd laid eyes on her. She unpinned her hat and handed that over, too.

"It's a very nice estate, my dear. Pleasant even in winter, although a tad chilly."

"Your blood has grown thin, living down south," Melza said. Gloucestershire wasn't exactly *north*, but it was a good deal colder in winter than Cornwall. It had taken her a few years to acclimatise when she'd first married.

"No doubt," her mother said. "Tea, Jonas."

The others trickled in behind her. Her father was out with her steward, inspecting drains, but several of her siblings were there. Not all, thank the Lord.

Melissa was in Vienna with Charles. Locryn and Elestryn were holding the fort at home, conducting all the traditional rituals for their tenants, but their children were here, fully occupied in snow-related games with the twins. It rarely snowed in Cornwall, so they were jubilant.

Petroc had brought his Beatrice. Dearest Felix had arrived from London yesterday with Kerenza, for her last Christmas as an unmarried woman, if she had her way.

Even Endellion was here, spending Christmas with the family for the first time in an age. He'd brought his Indian friend Mr

Arasan, a lovely fellow who was apparently the equivalent of a prince in his own country. Mr Arasan was just as intrigued by the snow as the children.

And Ives, of course, smiling at Katie in a nauseatingly loving way.

Oh, she was such a shrew! It was wonderful that those two were so in love. That *everyone* was so in love and happy.

Except her. Her and her aching back.

Jonas came back in with a silver salver of letters, followed by her butler, Bushell, with the tea tray. *He* was followed by a gaggle of maids bearing more trays, and she had to bite back a laugh. The way Bushell walked, with his chest thrown out, and the maids behind, looked so much like a mother duck leading her ducklings down to the pond.

"Would you pour, please, Mama?"

"Of course."

Jonas distributed the letters, and there was silence as they all went through their mail. Demelza had received half a dozen Christmas invitations which nobody expected her to accept, given her condition. In fact, they'd have been scandalised if she'd attended. Mama had a letter from Locryn. Kerenza, a note from Mr Muffet—really, she had to start calling him Val amongst the family, it was such a ridiculous name—which she passed across to Mama to read first, as per the family tradition. One was allowed to receive notes from a gentleman as long as Mama read them first.

She scowled down into her tea. She hadn't thought *much* about her mother's betrayal, but any reminder of it still stung.

"Oh dear." Katie sat wide-eyed, her letter in her lap.

"What is it, dear?" Mama asked.

"My mother…" Katie wet her lips nervously, and glanced up at Ives. "She says she doesn't want to be apart from me this first Christmas. So she's taken rooms in a hotel in Stroud. She's convinced Den to accompany her. She's here already."

There was silence. Everyone looked at Demelza.

"Katie, you know I'd invite her to stay here, but–" she began.

"Oh, no! There's no need." Katie's manner was earnest. "I *told* her there was no room, given that the Mandeville relations will be here for Christmas."

"We'll have to invite her to the Christmas dinner, though," Ives said gloomily. "No getting out of that."

"Ives!" Mama's tone was censorious, but he was just saying what they were all thinking.

"I'll write a note to her lodgings, if you furnish me with her address," Demelza said. "I'm sure we will be very glad to have her here for Christmas Eve and Christmas dinner."

"You're so kind!" Katie raised her chin, but Mel suspected it was to stop herself crying. "It's just like Mama to, to–"

"Weasel her way in," Ives finished. "And yes, Mama, I know that's not polite, but if you knew how long she'd stayed at Kirwich with us, despite copious hints that she'd outstayed her welcome, you'd be dashed glad there's no room here!"

Endellion gave a bark of laughter, and went out – no doubt, to the schoolroom to look for Sarah Lamb, despite that being a very bad idea.

She was positively *surrounded* by romances! Now, what was in that to make her want to cry? How she *hated* the emotional ups and downs of expecting!

DENZELL HANDED his mother down from the carriage. The light snow which had fallen the night before hadn't yet melted—really, it was far too early for a morning call! Mama had insisted.

He should have overridden her. Truth was, he wanted to see Mel as much as Mama wanted to see Katie. Or, rather, as much as she wanted to be included in the warmth of Trengrouse family life. It had been a long, lonely few months without Katie in the house; neither of them had realised how much *life* she'd put into everything.

Carefully, he steadied her up the slippery front steps and rang the bell.

The butler was expecting them, apparently. He ushered them in without a word, and gestured to a footman to take Den's gear while he helped Mama with her wraps and pelisse and gloves.

"The ladies are in the morning room." The butler led the way to a ground floor room which overlooked a rose garden, bare and cold, the roses packed in sacks to shield them from frost. The room itself was warm, papered in yellow and blue, light and bright. The ladies were making bows—red velvet, probably to put on the evergreen swags of Yuletide.

There she was. Good Lord, she was *huge*! Twins again?

Mel smiled up at both of them with practiced welcome. Did he imagine that she looked on him more warmly? "Welcome to Mandeville House, Lady Kelynack. Please forgive me for not getting up."

"Of course, my dear." Greetings were exchanged, and Kate came around the table to embrace Mama. The Countess nodded, Kerenza bobbed a curtsey. Hard to believe she was old enough to marry. She hadn't yet mastered her wild hair; it still escaped from its pins as it had when she was a schoolgirl.

It hit him how long he'd known everyone in this room. He made his way around to Mel and bent over her. Her head came up; did she think he was going to kiss her?

For a moment, their eyes met. How he wanted to. Desire for her churned in his belly; which was simply *wrong*, given that she was expecting another man's child. But he couldn't help it. He'd never been able to help anything, where Mel was concerned. Now he didn't have to hate her, there was nothing stopping him wanting her.

"Are you well?" he asked gently.

"Oh, I'm well enough." She gave a short laugh, and drew back a little. "This stage is all about having a bad back and a weak bladder."

He laughed too, and sat next to her. Mel had never minded her tongue around him; he was glad she still didn't.

"How long?"

"The midwife *says* New Year, but I think it's going to be earlier. I *hope* it will be!"

"Less than two weeks. You can survive that."

"Easy for you to say." They smiled at each other, and turned back to the group. Den's heart was light, as though it would float out of his chest. She was still his Mel; they were still friends. He could build on that.

DEMELZA WAS familiar with the surprisingly strong desires of pregnancy. She and John had enjoyed their marital pleasures right up until the twins came. The surge of desire she'd felt when Den had bent over her, though…that had shocked her. She was carrying her husband's child! It was, it was *outrageous* of her to be thinking of another man.

She'd never had any self-control where Den was concerned. In fact, if he hadn't been such a gentleman, she would have gone off to London with her maidenhood well and truly lost. He'd regulated both of them, always drawing back before they'd gone too far. It had been so frustrating! However, she'd been glad of it on her wedding night.

No need to worry about virginity when one was a mother to three children.

One of whom might be a boy.

That thought was like a bucket of cold water over her. Oh, why had he come? His mother could have come alone.

She listened politely to Lady Kelynack's description of their journey, arranged for their nuncheon, agreed with Kerenza's plan to get up a party to gather evergreens the next day. The perfect hostess.

All the while she was conscious of Den sitting next to her. Of his thigh, so close to the seat of her chair. Of his hands, long and strong, clasped on the table.

If he'd *had* to visit, why couldn't he have come when she wasn't so gravid? Early pregnancy was the perfect time for an affair. No chance of scandal from a widow falling pregnant, but with enough flexibility to enjoy oneself. Images of Den's hands on her flowed through her mind.

She flushed and pushed off the sofa, cutting off Lady Kelynack's questions to Kerenza about her beaus. The woman was being *so* nice, which was snide in itself.

"I'll just go to make sure everything is in readiness," she said, and walked out without specifying what had to be made ready. Perhaps the others would assume she needed the chamberpot.

Felix followed her, and stopped her with a hand on her arm, his hazel eyes full of brotherly concern.

"Make sure you look after yourself rather than looking after everyone else," he said. "If you have an errand, let me do it."

Her eyes filled with the ready tears of pregnancy. Dear Felix. "Oh, no. I just...I just–"

"Had had enough?" His mouth twisted in a wry smile. "I know the feeling. You're the hostess, Melza, but that doesn't mean you have to take everything that leech dishes out."

She blinked in surprise. Kind, gentle Felix calling Lady Kelynack a leech? Leech. Yes. That was how it felt, as though Lady Kelynack sucked the joy out of life; especially out of the lives of her children.

"I'll remember that." She patted his arm, and grinned. "Now I *must* go to the retiring room!"

He went ahead of her and opened the door. "I'll get your maid."

"Thank you," she said with real gratitude. She needed help to get up again from the commode. At least there *was* a commode, instead of just a chamber pot. She sat with a sigh of relief.

Ridiculous that the only peace she had these days was on the commode!

She should enjoy it while she could.

CHAPTER 9

Den adjusted the carriage rug over his mother's knees and tapped on the roof to tell the coachman to set off.

They crunched down the cleared drive easily; Melza's groundsmen kept the place spick and span, even in winter. It was a beautiful house; it would pain her to leave it, no doubt, if the baby was a girl.

His mother was unusually bright, sitting upright and smiling. "Well, it's clear that Demelza is well settled in this house."

"She may still have to leave it."

Mother frowned. "Nonsense! She's carrying high. I'm sure it will be a boy. And even if it's a girl, she'll want her children brought up around their heritage. The Dower House is perfectly suitable for her."

The Dower House on their own land was a large and very comfortable place, but he didn't think Mother would be so complacent about being forced to live there. She continued talking about the afternoon's events with energy, clearly having enjoyed the company.

Was she lonely?

He'd never considered that before. She had many visiting acquaintances in Cornwall, and was out from morning until night most days.

Perhaps she didn't like coming home to an empty house, now Katie was gone.

When she fell silent, he ventured, "Mother, have you considered hiring a companion? Someone to keep you company when I'm out on the estate?"

Startled, she reared back in dismay. "A

companion? So *you* don't need to keep me company? Don't need to ever *see* me? A sop to your conscience while you go haring off after women?" Her voice rose in the familiar, anguished tones. She scrubbed at her eyes with her kerchief, hiccuping sobs. "I know you don't love me, not the way a boy should love his mother, but I hoped you wouldn't fob me off on some *stranger*! A *stranger*, Denzell!"

And off she went. Scolding, sobbing, begging…

Normally, when she went into one of these flights, she'd storm off, or Den would placate her.

He found he wasn't in the mood to placate. It had been a perfectly reasonable suggestion, born out of his genuine concern for her. She was being—she was being ridiculous.

For a moment, she took the handkerchief away from her face.

He'd be damned if he could see a single tear. He suddenly realised that her habit of

running off was a deuced good way of con-
cealing a lack of actual crying. Being caught
in the carriage with him had revealed her.

The cunning old besom…but then he saw
the look in her eyes, and it full of true mis-
ery. And fear.

"There's no need to be upset, Mother," he
sighed. "It was only a suggestion."

She pushed him to apologise, and he said
a few things to quieten her. Unlike similar
past episodes, he said them without guilt.

He hadn't been in the wrong at all.

How many times had that been true in
the past? How many times had she convinced him that he'd been unkind, or selfish,
or hard-hearted?

Too many.

THE NEXT DAY was Christmas Eve, and
Kerenza took the children and most of the
adults out gathering greenery to decorate the
house with.

Melza was restless. She recognised the

instinct to "nest"; with luck, that meant the baby would come soon. Not much she could do around the house, so she set off walking to the Dower House, with her mother as company.

The walk might bring on the baby, too. She crossed her fingers.

It was odd, but she'd noticed before that it was easier to walk while pregnant than stand. She enjoyed the crisp air even though the lowering clouds threatened more snow. At least the children would enjoy it.

The Dower House was older than the main house by almost a hundred years; John's father had built the main house just after he was born, but the Dower House had parts going back to the Tudors, although most of it was William and Mary.

"A little dark," her mother said, inspecting the main reception room which, in the country fashion, was on the ground floor. Small windows and deep walls meant that the temperature inside was better than outside, but it was hardly enticing.

"Yes." Melza surveyed the furniture. Hard backed settles and upright chairs, all looking drearily uncomfortable. The enormous fireplace would eat up wood, and the inglenook was attractive, but impractical to modern eyes.

She sighed. "I can afford to refurnish. New drapes, new sofas, a closed stove in the kitchen…"

"The ceilings are low." They were. Dark beams hung above their heads like ranked Swords of Damocles.

"Are you *trying* to make me dislike it, Mama?"

Her mother dimpled. "I must admit, I'd rather you were home with us."

Dread lodged in her stomach, startling her. Would it be so bad? Her heart sped up in answer. *Yes*.

She loved her family, but there were so *many* of them! After her quiet life with John and the twins, it was all too much.

If this baby were a girl…no, going back to Trengrouse Hall to live wasn't the answer.

She just wished she knew what was.

"I think I'll buy a house in London," she said without thinking. It would do as a plan for now. One never lost money by buying in London.

"Buy? Can you afford that?"

She grinned. "I certainly can. I'm swimming in lard!"

"Demelza!" her mother said in reproof. "Such language!" But she was smiling. "We shall find you something suitable to buy, then."

"Unless it's a boy."

A boy with John's eyes and strong chin. That would be lovely. *John* would want that so much, for his son to take over Mandeville House and estate. She had to want it too, for his sake.

"Unless it's a boy," Mama agreed gently, and took her arm as they continued on their inspection tour.

. . .

Demelza greeted John's cousin and his wife when they arrived, showing them to the best guest room, which she had reserved for them, given that they might be the owners of the house by the time they left. Their sons had taken advantage of Napoleon's defeat and were off in the south of France on a sailing holiday, so at least she didn't have to deal with them. They did *gaze* at one so!

Mrs Mandeville looked around and grudgingly nodded. Clearly she'd have been offended by any lesser suite. George Mandeville, a small, mousy man, smiled at her with gratitude. Had he thought she'd stick them in the coal cellar?

No use tip-toeing around the truth.

She patted her abdomen. "We'll know soon where we all stand."

Mrs Mandeville took in a sharp breath. "That's hardly a subject fit for discussion in mixed company."

Lord, they were bourgeois! John had been a gentleman and was welcomed in Society, but even he had commented occasionally on the "free and easy ways" of the nobility in which she'd been raised.

"We're all family here," Melza said soothingly.

She left them to unpack, with a maid to see to Mrs Mandeville. Another strike against the Dower House; she'd be expected to dine *en famille* with these two regularly, and she wasn't at all sure she could do it. Not without offending that woman.

THE GARLAND-GATHERING PARTY had returned in triumph, Den included, all weighed down by green boughs, and immediately began decorating. By dinnertime, when his mother arrived, the house was adorned with greenery and smelt like a pine forest.

Lady Kelynack and Mrs Mandeville took one look at each other and discovered an arch enemy. Strange, he'd have thought they'd get on. They were similar in so many ways: age and gentility and a tendency to criticise… Perhaps it was the recognition that they *were* similar that had set up Mama's back. She didn't like to be reminded that she'd married "up" when she became Lady Kelynack. Her own father had been a mere "Mister".

With all of the Trengrouses there, it was like a Society party. Especially when Endellion stalked in, accompanied by a very *point-device* Indian man. A Mr Arasan. Den had never seen such perfect tailoring; it made even Felix, the nattiest among them, look slightly sloppy.

On introduction, Mother favoured Mr Arasan with a cold nod and a turned shoulder. No curtsey. Should he reprove her, or would that make it worse? He shook Arasan's hand heartily to make up for it, and discovered a knowing humour in the man's eyes which made him flush with mortification.

They fell into conversation, most properly, about the weather, and the fact that Arasan had never seen snow up close before, living as he did in the southern Indian city of Tanjore.

They'd brushed through it pretty well, Den thought, but then it came time to sit at table.

They'd put his mother next to Arasan. Of course they had. As the wife and daughters of an earl, every woman present, except Mrs Mandeville, outranked her, and Arasan was a mere Mister, so ranked below all the Trengrouse men, who were Honourables.

The footman pulled her chair out, but she stood, glaring in disbelief as Arasan came to the neighbouring chair.

She swivelled to Demelza.

"Melza Trengrouse, how *dare* you put me next to this-this *man*?"

Arasan stiffened, but remained silent. Den could feel the blood drain from his face, and he gazed at Demelza, hoping for—what? Some magic solution which would appease Mother without insulting Arasan?

Not possible.

Clearly Demelza didn't think so.

"Lady Kelynack," she said, her face cold and her voice crisp. "I fear you are under a misapprehension. Firstly, my name, as you well know, is Lady Demelza Mandeville, and I would thank you to use it. Secondly, Mr Arasan is an honoured guest in this house, and I will brook no disrespect to him. Please apologise."

His heart surged. She was magnificent! But it wouldn't end well.

"*Apologise*? To a–a–"

"Be very careful what you say next, Lady Kelynack."

Every person at the table was frozen, except Felix, who looked back and forward between the two with an air of appreciative interest, and Endellion, who rose from his seat and took two paces to stand at Arasan's shoulder. Arasan himself was as composed as if they were all discussing the weather.

He had to say something.

"Mother–" he began.

"I will *not* apologise! It is *you* who should

apologise to *me* for placing me in this impossible position!"

Mrs Mandeville nodded. Clearly Mr Arasan wouldn't be invited here if she was the hostess.

"Mother–"

"Then I'm afraid you must leave, Lady Kelynack."

"There's no need–" Arasan said.

"There is every need." Melza flicked a glance to the footman. "Jonas, please fetch Lady Kelynack's wraps."

Mother's face was red with rage and embarrassment. "You can't seriously–I'm one of your mother's oldest friends!"

The countess waved a hand. "Don't bring me into this, Margaret. You've crossed the line." The sheer boredom in her tone was astonishing, and appeared to genuinely upset his mother.

The earl, seated at the head of the table, shook his head. "Bad form, Margaret. Dashed bad form."

"I–"

"Goodbye, Lady Kelynack." Melza's voice was diamond sharp. Gods, she was wonderful! He tried to show how he felt with his eyes, but she turned away.

Had she expected *him* to intervene? Well, he'd *tried.*

He could have tried harder.

When the footman came with the wraps, he helped his mother into them with firm hands, and shrugged into his own coat.

"I'm sorry, Lady Demelza," he said, "but I do have to escort my mother home."

"Of course you do." Her voice was flat. Was there a slight curl to her lip? He burned with shame, but he bowed low before ushering his mother out.

In the carriage, it started.

"How *dare* that woman—" And she was off like a horse in a race.

Not this time. He cut in without listening to a word.

"No, Mother." She stopped mid-sentence,

then drew breath to remonstrate. "*No*, Mother. You were wrong. Simply wrong."

"That man–"

There was no use giving his mother a sermon about all God's children being equal. She only went to church for the socialising. He had to use an argument she'd accept.

"That man was a guest at your hostess's table. You had a social duty to act accordingly. I–I was ashamed of you."

She gasped. And then cried.

Real tears, silent, pouring down her stricken face.

Something twisted under his heart, but he kept his face stern. As though she were a child; and really, her inability to control her emotions *was* like a child.

"Tomorrow, you should write a note of apology, and I'll take it up for you."

At least that would give him an excuse to see Melza and apologise in person.

"I shall *not*."

He regarded her sombrely. "I think you

will, if you don't wish to be alone over Christmas."

Fear flickered in her eyes. The prospect of being alone…those dark days after his father's death reared up in his mind. "I'm *alone*," she had wailed, over and over, until he had sworn, promised, that he'd stay with her, that she'd never be alone…

That fear was real, and deep, and apparently would never go away.

He was stuck in a terrible combination of pity and exasperation. How much of his life, of Katie's life, had been shadowed by her desperate need to be *with* someone?

Compassion made him pat her hand.

"It will be all right, Mother. But you must write that apology."

She clutched his hand in hers as though he were five again.

"You're a good boy, Denzell," she whispered.

In her eyes, he would never grow up. He shouldn't see himself through her gaze; he'd never break free if he did.

With sudden shame, he remembered the prank he'd played on Ives last summer, sending him out in the cove in a boat he'd taken the bung out of, knowing he'd have to swim for it. A schoolboy prank, his mother had called it, laughing, but he was no schoolboy. He'd felt quite at home, having a man nine years younger than he as a best friend after Petroc went on campaign to the Peninsula, but surely that wasn't right, even if he'd known Ives his whole life? Well, Ives' whole life.

He should be married with children by now. *Ives* was more grown up than he!

He'd used Demelza's supposed betrayal as an excuse not to mature, and that was the truth. Whereas she, far more adult, had married and mothered and become the woman she was meant to be.

Underneath the shame, though, was the knowledge that part of his reluctance to woo and marry some pretty young thing was the knowledge of how his mother would react. It had just been *easier* to let the years go by…

No more.

Goddammit, no more.

The question was, did Demelza still care for him? Was there any chance at all that they could resume their interrupted courtship? Did he still feel the same way about her; or she about him?

He would find out. Tomorrow.

CHAPTER 10

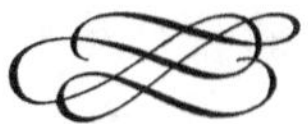

*D*emelza's back was slightly better today.

"Hmm," her mother said. "That baby is ready to be born."

After eight living births and one stillbirth, she would know.

At last! Melza sent for the month nurse, Mrs Griffiths. A shame to spoil the woman's Christmas, but she'd be well paid, and better to have her here a day or so early…just in case.

Melza went about the morning's exchange of small gifts and treats for the children with a light heart. Not only was this pregnancy coming to an end, but she didn't have to deal with Lady Kelynack at Christmas dinner.

Poor Den! He'd be having a shocking time of it, no doubt. Part of her felt sorry for him; the other part wanted to tap him on the head as you would a naughty spaniel and say, "Serve you right!" He should have stood up to that woman years ago.

On the other hand…as she sipped eggnog and watched through the library window at the children sledding down the back hill, she was rather glad he hadn't. If he had, he would have been married by now.

A tickle of pleasure that he wasn't made her frown. This was hardly the time to think about other men.

As though the thought brought it on, a labour pain rippled across her belly. Not just the spasms of false labour which she'd been experiencing for weeks. This was the real thing.

Finally! And birthing one child *must* be

easier than birthing two, surely? No need to alarm the others, but she would get Jonas immediately to take the carriage for the midwife, rather than waiting for her to arrive under her own steam. At least she'd made her will; the girls would be brought up at Trengrouse Hall, and if a son survived and she didn't, the Mandevilles would raise him here, on his ancestral inheritance, so he would know his land and people, and they would know him. It pained her to think of the twins separated from their brother, but Mama would make sure they spent time together.

Thinking of her own death made her grief for John blossom, but she had no time to be low. After sending Jonas off, she made a careful way to the second drawingroom, which had been set aside as the lying-in room, since it had an anteroom where the family could gather. The birthing cot was there already, and an old-fashioned birthing stool which her midwife swore by; it had certainly made the twins' births easier.

She was grateful that they were in the snows of Gloucestershire; she'd never liked the idea of a male accoucheur, but in London it was *de rigeur*. Old Mrs Swindon was better. Experienced and with a kind tongue which kept the atmosphere light.

Best to keep moving. She went to the kitchen and ordered the caudle to be made. The hot spiced wine was for both her and the waiting family.

Her cook beamed at her. "I have it all ready to be heated, my lady! God bless you and the little one."

"Thank you, Cook." All the staff gathered round, and she smiled at them.

"Well, we'll know soon if I stay with you or go," she said. "So I'd like to say now how grateful I am to all of you for your service to me and to the master. He was fond of you all, as I am."

"If it's a girl, my lady, would you be setting up your own establishment?" her butler asked.

She hesitated. "Yes, eventually. But it

would be a much smaller house than this." The butler and cook exchanged glances, and the cook pursed her lips. She couldn't steal her staff away from the Mandevilles. Could she? That would be *wonderful!*

"We'll see how things go, shall we? No need to make decisions yet."

As the butler walked her out and helped her up the stairs to the lying-in room, she said, "You wouldn't be happy in a small house, Bushell."

He sniffed. "I'm feeling my age, my lady. A smaller house might suit me very well. Under the right mistress."

Tears rose to her eyes. The staff's loyalty felt like a cushion she could fall onto when things were too hard. How silly of her!

No, loyalty was never silly.

"I'd welcome any of the staff who wanted to come," she said. "But you should know I don't intend on moving to the Dower House."

"We thought you might not, my lady."

He handed her into a chair and bowed, lower than normal, then left.

A moment later the pain hit again, and she let her head fall back against the chair. She'd forgotten how much it hurt.

Bushell would organise everything from now on. Inform the family, send her maid with linens and the birthing chemise and petticoat, serve the caudle…all she had to do was give birth.

The rest of her life was hanging in the balance. To stay at Mandeville House, with a son and the twins, or to leave with three daughters.

She just wanted to *know*. Now! More than that, she wanted to *control* how and where she lived, not have it depend on the sex of a baby.

How hard it was to be a woman.

DEN HAD WRESTED the apology out of his mother and left her after the hotel's

Christmas meal, held, as tradition demanded, in the middle of the day.

The ride up to Mandeville House wasn't long, but it was damned cold. His hired horse's breath left plumes of steam in the air; he kept his face muffled in a thick scarf, but even under his hat the tips of his ears were freezing.

He rode around to the stables to leave his horse, and found the grooms toasting Demelza.

"Her ladyship be lying-in," the head groom told him, ruddy with Christmas beer. "And she have sent us summat to drink her health."

Lying in.

He tipped the groom and went into the house through the kitchen door; not quite the done thing, but surely he knew the Trengrouses well enough, if not the Mandevilles?

There was no one in the downstairs drawingroom, but sound came from upstairs. Convivial sound.

He followed it to a smallish reception

room where the Mandevilles and most of the Trengrouses were drinking hot wine. Was that a custom? He'd never been to a lying-in before. At least the children weren't there.

The earl saw him and his brows twitched together in a quick frown, but once he saw that he was alone, he smiled.

"Not long now," he said. "God willing."

From the next room came a moan of pain, and every woman there winced; every man took a swig of the wine.

"That doesn't sound good," Den said. He wanted to go in, but of course he couldn't. Only the father was welcome in the lying-in room.

The earl waved a hand. "It hurts," he said simply. "Maria sounded like that every time, and it hasn't been long. Only a few hours. Can take all night sometimes."

His eyes were clouded with memories; Den recalled that at least one of the Trengrouse babies had been stillborn. He and Petroc had been around twelve then.

The door to the lying-in room opened and the countess came out. Everyone swivelled towards her. She smiled, but it was strained.

"It will be some time," she said. "Demelza has suggested that you go about normal life, and we'll call you when the time is nearer."

"We don't mind keeping vigil," Felix said.

"She doesn't want you to, my dear. I think…" The countess hesitated. "I think the noise of conversation is bothering her."

There was more to it than that. He knew his Mel. She never liked to show weakness. Making a noise where they could all hear her would mortify her. And they said it was better for the woman if she let the pain out.

He went up to the countess. "Could you tell her that I have an apology written by my mother? I know it's not that important right now, but it might take one problem away from her mind."

The countess patted his arm. "I'll tell her. That was well done."

They all trooped down to the draw-ingroom, except the earl who slid off to the library with some muttered excuse.

Outside, the children and Mr Arasan were playing in the snow with Miss Lamb, the governess. Endellion went out with them.

Petroc came over to sit by him, wine in hand, and Den gave him the apology to be passed on in due course. They hadn't had much chance to talk on this visit, although of course he'd seen plenty of Petroc and his new bride back in Swain Cove. They grate-fully fell into a conversation about the horse stud she and Petroc were creating, and the mares he had in foal.

A stifled noise came from upstairs, and Den stopped in the middle of a sentence.

"It's not her first," Petroc said uneasily. "I'm sure she'll be fine."

There was no guarantee of that. Women died in childbirth all the time. Often. Or af-terwards, from childbed fever. His hand clenched on the arm of the chair.

A world without Demelza was…it was *impossible*. Impossible that he could be in a world and she not share it.

He had wondered if he would still feel the same way; the twist of his heart, the curdle in his bowels showed him that it was worse than that: he felt *more*. Far more. She had been a lovely girl. As a woman, she was incomparable.

He couldn't bear not knowing.

An hour went past. Two.

The early winter night was beginning to draw in. If he was going back to Stroud, he had to leave now.

He couldn't leave without seeing her. Without knowing how it was going. He wasn't sure he could leave at all.

The countess came in, looking worried, and went to speak privily to the earl. Now was his chance. He made his goodbyes, which were perfunctorily acknowledged, and set off up the stairs.

But there was a woman in the anteroom drinking water, and he already knew the other door to the corridor was locked. A superstition to keep out bad spirits.

He couldn't just burst in. The scandal! At the very least, people would wonder if the child was his. He couldn't do that to Demelza —or to John and the baby.

Reluctantly, he turned to go, when a scream echoed down the corridor. The woman whisked herself inside.

He had to *see* her. But he couldn't.

His steps dragging, he went out through the kitchen. The cook was huddled with the butler, and he caught the words, "Looking bad, they say." They were both pale, with worried brows.

His stomach clenched. He might never see her again.

The lying-in room was at the back of the house. The old section, with all its crenellations and carvings. He looked up at it. Candles lit the window panes of only one room. That must be it. Damn it. He just had to *see* her. He shrugged off his driving coat and began to climb.

. . .

THIS WAS FAR WORSE than the twins.

"It's a biggun," the midwife said, patting her shoulder. "Prolly a boy. Boys come bigger."

The month nurse sniffed. "I've seen some sizeable girls in my time. And my lady is tall."

"Aye…" the midwife gripped Demelza's hands as another pain hit. "Breathe it out and scream if you want to, my duck. No one to hear you but us."

Melza gasped and choked and moaned as the pain seemed to go on forever.

Katie mopped her brow. She had insisted on being present, "To learn," she said, "as I'm expecting myself now. It's early days, but I'm reasonably sure."

The midwife and the month nurse were talking in a corner. They looked worried. That was bad. They were both very experienced.

"It is breech?" she managed to ask.

"Aye, maybe," the midwife said. "We'll wait a little longer and then I'll try to turn it."

Breech. Where the bottom came out first instead of the head. Far more likely to kill her.

She might die tonight.

A sharp pain pierced her, but it wasn't a labour pain. She wished, so much, that she and Den could have had some time together before…They hadn't managed even a single word in private. Damn this family, and his! There were too many people in this house. If only she could have seen him, for just a moment.

She did love him so. Still, and again, and forever. She had loved John. Yet Denzell remained the beloved of her soul, no matter what. If only she'd had the chance to tell him that…

Something banged on the window, and she jumped. Katie sprang to her feet, the other women spun to look.

"Den!" Katie gasped. She ran to the window and opened it.

Good Lord, it *was* Den! Despite her weariness, she began to laugh.

"I just want to see her," his voice came, pleading.

"Let him in," she croaked, just as another pain swept over her.

She lost time and all sense of place for a few moments. The pains were getting worse; longer and less time in between.

When she came back to herself, he was there, blue eyes dark with concern.

"My own love, I had to see you."

My own love. *That* was what she'd needed. She grasped his hand.

"I'm glad you came."

Something in his face changed; was that relief?

"Out!" the midwife ordered.

"And keep your mouth shut about having been in here at all!" the month nurse declared.

"It would be better if you left now, Den. Before the countess comes back."

That got him moving. He rose and

pressed a kiss into Melza's knuckles. "I'll see you tomorrow. You and the babe."

She nodded, somehow smiling. He drew back from her slowly, reluctantly, but there was a noise at the door and that sent him out the window in a hurry, reminding her of the boy she'd known so well. Chuckling, heart somehow lighter, she put a hand on her abdomen. "Come now, child. Time to make your appearance."

The midwife checked between her legs. "Aye. It's breech. Time for the birthing chair. I'll be able to get a better grip there."

Her mother was there. "You'll be fine, Melza," she said with confidence. "You have my hips."

That made her giggle. Perhaps she'd had too much of the caudle herself. Katie gave her some water and they all helped her to the birthing chair.

It was like the start of a hunt, anticipation laced with fear of what might be.

Tally Ho!

. . .

Den rode back to Stroud through the gathering night, praying harder than he'd ever prayed before.

CHAPTER 11

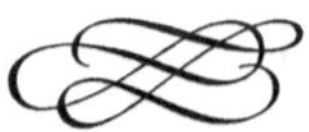

*D*en arrived at daybreak the next morning. The family were just rising from breakfast, with set, pale faces.

"Still?" he asked Petroc.

"They say 'soon'," he answered, "but they've been saying that for an hour." He hit his thigh with a closed fist. "It's a good deal easier going into battle than waiting around for this!"

They adjourned to the drawingroom and sat, none of them speaking much. Even the Mandevilles had caught the general anxiety, although Mrs Mandeville sent him suspicious glances.

He had no rights to even be here. Thank God the Trengrouses understood that he and Melza were *friends*, if nothing else. Another family would have shown him the door.

He spared one brief thought for his mother, but she'd brought her isolation on herself, and he couldn't feel sorry for her.

"PUSH!" the midwife said. "He's all ready to come."

He. Damn it. Her breath was shallow and she was so *tired*. How did this martinet expect her to *push*? If she pushed, her heart would burst.

The pain rolled over her and, her mother's hand on her shoulders, encouraging words in her ears, she pushed.

And again.

And again. It hurt so much.

"Come on, my duck, you can do it." But the midwife's voice was worried.

How big could this baby possibly *be*?

Another push. Then, suddenly, relief. The oddest sensation as it slid out.

"She's weak," the midwife muttered. There was the sound of a light slap, and a feeble cry.

She?

"A girl," Mama said with satisfaction. "A girl, Melza. You're free."

Free. Yes! She hadn't known Mama understood. She hadn't realised herself how badly she'd wanted a girl. Her world expanded around her as she reached out for the baby. Anything was possible now. She could go anywhere. Do anything.

"One more push," the midwife said.

This one wasn't hard, although she was exhausted. Then they cut the cord, wrapped the babe and delivered her into Melza's arms. Her darling girl. She had John's fair hair, and she *was* a tall one.

"Joanna," Melza said. "For John. Joanna Mary." Her mother's face lit up. Although Papa always called her Maria, her actual name was Mary. A peace offering, of sorts. She hadn't quite forgiven her mother for her interference, but she understood it.

"Joanna Mary," Katie said. "I'll tell the others." She sounded exhausted. She'd been a tower of strength over the whole ordeal.

"Thank you, Katie," Melza managed, and then her eyes closed as she felt the midwife and month nurse begin to clean her up. No wetnurse. The Trengrouse women suckled their own babies, and bedamned to what Society thought!

Before she slid into sleep, one last thought made her smile: she would get to show Denzell her new little lady.

"She's delivered of a girl," Katie said. "Joanna Mary. Demelza is exhausted, but the midwife says there's no cause to worry."

Den let out a shaky breath as there were cheers all round. She would be all right. She would *live*. His own love.

"We need the wassail cup!" the earl declared.

Indeed they did.

CHAPTER 12

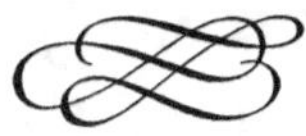

After Christmas, the party began to break up. Sarah Lamb left, secretly, with Mr Arasan, after saying goodbye to Demelza. She thought Sarah had chosen well: a marriage between an illegitimate governess and the Honourable Endellion Trengrouse...well, she had no guilt over having spirited the girl away, no matter how Endellion scowled at her.

The Mandevilles left too, to go back to their own home to pack and get ready to move to Mandeville House. George Mandeville kept his glee hidden, but his wife had less self-control, and no doubt had toured the house with great satisfaction.

She'd have less satisfaction, perhaps, when she realised how many of the objet d'arts were Demelza's personal property. And pretty much all of the jewellery, John's mother not having had a taste for it. Fortunately, there was an inventory.

Melza dozed most of the week, with Mrs Griffiths the month-nurse standing guard. Her parents were leaving on New Year's Day, with Petroc and Beatrice and Kerenza. Thank God Beatrice and Katie were long-time friends of the family, and she hadn't had to be the Society hostess for them. Felix had gone off on Boxing Day to his ochre mine.

Until New Year's, the house was in Mama's capable hands, and she could simply recover and enjoy her little darling. The girls barely left her side. They were entranced by Joanna, and competed to hold her and bathe her.

"It's only natural," Mrs Griffiths the

month-nurse said indulgently. "It's how they learn to be mothers."

Lord knew, she had learnt the same way, looking after her younger siblings—and even her older ones, when they'd needed a sensible sister.

Mama came to see her often, but the rest of the household were excluded by the month nurse. "At least a week," she said firmly, but she did allow the baby to be shown around by Mama.

It was so peaceful. She was still in pain, and bleeding a little, but she didn't have to bestir herself, or make any decisions, although that would come soon. It was the first time in her life that she hadn't wanted to *organise* things.

She tried not to think about Denzell, because doing so brought up a maelstrom of feeling: love, happiness, bitterness, fear for the future. Every time his face came to mind, she heard her mother's voice: *Do you honestly think Denzell Kelynack would have made his mother leave her home?*

She just didn't believe he would. Which meant there was no future for them, because she'd be damned before she lived with that woman.

DENZELL VISITED DAILY, but got no further than the front parlour.

"You can't go up, Den," Petroc said. "And if you keep trying, you'll start a scandal."

Beatrice patted his arm. "She's fine. I've seen her, and there's no danger. No fever."

He had to be content with that.

His mother was insisting on having his escort back to Cornwall, and he'd run out of excuses. He'd take her back and then return. Mel had been glad he'd climbed up to her window. She'd smiled when he called her his own love. Surely that meant they had a chance?

On the other hand, she'd been in the middle of childbirth, and half out of her mind with pain. There was no certainty, except that he loved her.

. . .

ON NEW YEAR'S EVE, Mama said, "I assume that you'll come back to the Hall as soon as you've recovered enough. Leave this place to the Mandevilles." Perhaps she looked askance, because her mother added hastily, "If you don't want to live with us, you could rent a house in the neighbourhood. Swain Cove, perhaps, near Beatrice's mother."

Swain Cove. It was a pretty little town, right on the sea. She had friends there. Beatrice, and Charity Penhaligon…

The sea.

Oh, how she missed the ocean! The sound of it at night, the scent of salt on the breeze, the freedom of taking a sailboat out on a fine day…London couldn't compare.

"Yes," she said. "Yes. Swain Cove is a good idea." She smiled at her mother and kissed the top of Joanna's head, taking in that milky baby smell. And then she cried, overtaken with tears because Joanna would never know her father.

"Ah," Mrs Griffiths said, wiping her face as though she were a child, "her milk's come in. She'll do fine now."

THE NEXT DAY she insisted on getting up, her legs as wobbly as a new-born lamb's.

New Year's Day. The start of a new life.

She settled into the drawingroom sofa with a wince, and held out her arms for Joanna. Mrs Griffiths crooned, "There she is, the beautiful girl," and let her go reluctantly, and Nanny, who had been excluded from her bedroom, pounced.

There'd be a battle royal between these two pretty soon, but the lines were clearly drawn: the month nurse had the baby for a month and not a day more, and then she was all Nanny's.

It seemed right that Denzell should knock as soon as Nanny had resettled the baby in her arms.

Katie and Beatrice were both there, and

welcomed him in terms which made it clear he'd called every day.

That warmed her. He looked tired, too. A little older.

"Come and see my girl, Den," she said.

He sat next to them and touched the back of his finger to Joanna's cheek. She turned her head towards it, expecting the breast, and Melza chuckled at her pout when there was nothing there for her to suckle.

"She's beautiful." Den's voice croaked as if with strong emotion. Why on Earth? He cleared his throat. "I–we were worried."

"It wasn't an easy birth," she allowed.

"Which is why you mustn't stay up too long," Mrs Griffiths said, standing. But Nanny stood too, and took the woman's arm.

"She's fine where she is for the moment. Come and I'll show you the portrait of her when she was a wee thing. The spit and image of her mother, that babe is!"

Nanny frogmarched Mrs Griffiths out the door, with a significant glance at the girls. Katie smiled and rose, pulling Bea along with her.

"I'd like to see this portrait," she said.

So they were alone.

"It's a total lie," Melza said. "Joanna is the spit of her father, not me."

"Mel…"

Sudden tears came to her eyes.

"Not now, Den. I can't think of anything but Joanna now."

He drew back. "I understand. I–I just want you to know how much I love you. Just that." Their gazes met, and held.

A thunderous knock on the door startled both of them.

Bushell opened it and Lady Kelynack sailed straight past him and into the drawingroom.

"I knew it! I knew I'd find you here–"

"Saying farewell to our hostess, as I should," Den said. He stood protectively over Melza.

She really wasn't up to this. But it had to happen sometime, and perhaps it was better to know exactly where she stood? Before she made plans.

THE COUNTESS HURRIED IN, her mouth tight, her eyes furious. Denzell took a step back, but stayed close to Melza. He couldn't let his mother bully her.

"Margaret, this isn't the time for social visits. It's Demelza's first time out of the bedroom."

"And she's dallying with my boy!"

"Oh, for Heaven's sake! You talk as though he were a child! He's almost thirty!"

Yet again he was letting someone else argue for him. Like a child in truth. No more.

"Mother, there's no need for you to be here."

"There's every need if that hussy is inveigling you into marriage! If you think I'll share a house with her–"

"No," he interrupted. "I don't. Which is

why you'll have to leave, if Demelza is gracious enough to marry me."

There was dead silence. Mother looked as though he'd struck her. A pang of guilt hit him, but he pushed it down. An odd feeling of freedom took its place.

"I have no expectation of that," he added, looking at Melza. "Just hopes."

Without speaking, she slid her free hand up into his. But her eyes were shining.

Mother got her voice back. "I will not live in that Dower House! I will *not*–

Her voice was climbing, turning into a shriek. In the past, that would have made him give in, the memory of her poised in the open window overshadowing his whole life.

Not now. He no longer believed she was unbalanced, unless it was unbalanced to be totally selfish.

"No," he said again. "Not the Dower House. I'll buy you a house of your own. Bath would be a good idea, don't you think? You used to enjoy going there every year with Father."

Her mouth opened and closed. *"Bath?"* Then she rallied. "What if she doesn't marry you? Do you think I'll forget this?"

For a long moment, Melza held her breath. This was the real test. Was he standing up to his mother just to clear the way for *her*, or had he really grown up and taken responsibility for his own life? Was he the boy she remembered, or a man she could lean on? Lean on as she'd never dared lean on John.

Den laughed bitterly. "I think you'll remember this to your dying day, and try to make me pay for it just as long. Whether Melza marries me or not, I want you out of the house. You can decide where you want to live. Bath, or London, or somewhere else, I don't care. Just not with me."

Yes!

"And not with Katie and Ives," her mother added quickly. "They'd prefer their privacy too."

Good fielding, Mama!

All the colour had drained from Lady Kelynack's face. There was true fear there, and panic.

"I'll be *alone*," she said, as though it were death staring her in the face.

"Invite Amanda Beasley to live with you," Den said. "You're thick as thieves anyway. She'd love it. You know how cheeseparing she is, she'd be delighted to put the expenses of the household onto you."

"*Amanda Beasley*," she replied with scorn. "A woman!"

"In Bath," Melza said, deliberately coolly, "you can find yourself a new husband."

That got through. Lady Kelynack blinked, as though it were a completely new idea. Her face rearranged itself and Melza could see the prettier, younger woman she had known before Den's father had died. She hadn't been so…so *much*, back then.

"I've never been so insulted," Lady Kelynack said, but it was without conviction. She seemed dazed. Mama took her in hand.

"Come and have tea in the morning

room," she said. "We'll plan your trip to Bath to find a house. How exciting it will be!"

The woman blinked again, and colour began to return to her cheeks. "I won't be fobbed off with somewhere unfashionable," she warned. "The Royal Crescent would be appropriate."

"Quite, my dear," her mother agreed, shutting the door behind them.

Before she could draw breath, Nanny bounced back into the room, snatched Joanna from her, and bounced out again.

Melza laughed helplessly.

"This entire household seems to be colluding to leave us alone. It's quite improper."

"You're a respectable widow," he said, sitting again and kissing her hand. "You're allowed to receive suitors alone."

Didn't he understand? Her whole life was in chaos. She was choked with gratitude that he had laid down the law to his mother, but...how could she make plans? How could she not, when he stared at her with those eyes, so full of love? A lifelong love.

"It's not a year since John—"

He put a finger on her lips. "I know, Mel. Of course I know. You're in mourning. You need more time, and so do I, to adjust to running my own life. But…we could have an understanding."

THAT AMUSED HER, her lips quirking in that half-smile he knew so well. "An understanding? And just what would we understand?"

"That we love one another. And, when the time is ripe, we will marry. Will you marry me then, Demelza Trengrouse?"

He waited, not afraid. They were meant to be together, and both of them knew it.

"No," she said. His heart gave a great thump, and seemed to stop. "No, Demelza Trengrouse won't marry you, because I'm not that person anymore. But Demelza Mandeville will. In eighteen months or so, when I'm out of black gloves."

Happiness broke over him as he bent to kiss her.

They had kissed, and more, when they were young. This was different. Not just exciting, but lapped in love; full of promise, full of desire, full of joy.

DEN'S MOUTH on hers was better than she remembered. Strong and beautiful, his hands cupping her face, his lips gentle but full of need.

Even as tired as she was, she desired him. Not that *that* was possible right now. The thought made her wince, and he drew back in alarm.

"I've hurt you!"

"No, no…but I think we should leave it at that until I'm fully recovered."

"Of course! I'm sorry–"

She gurgled with laughter, for the first time feeling like the girl who had gone off to her first Season with such assurance that he'd be coming for her.

He'd come for her this time, and she'd meet him halfway.

"Eighteen months," she said. "I was considering renting in Swain Cove. Do you think that's a good idea?" Making decisions together, as they used to. Only at this very moment did she realise how heavy the burden of being the only decision-maker had been.

"An excellent idea. It will give my mother time to buy a house and move out without causing gossip."

"Maybe you could find a house for me?" Could she let someone else choose her house? Yes, if it was Den. He knew her so well, he would know what she'd like; and they'd always had the same tastes.

"I'd be happy to." He did look happy! "No one will be surprised," he added. "Everyone always knew how much I loved you." He twinkled at her, and kissed the tip of each finger. "And how much you *swooned* over me!"

She pushed him. "Denzell Kelynack! Are you saying I was *obvious*?"

"Smelling of April and May, the both of us."

"We always will," she said, and he kissed her lightly, so lightly, again.

They had time for more. The rest of their lives.

"Always," he said.

And then the twins ran in and Nanny followed, carrying Joanna, and all the rest of the family too, beaming knowingly at them.

This was home, and Swain Cove would be home, and she and Den would make a new home with the three girls at Kelynack House, and with any other children they were blessed with.

Together.

AUTHOR'S NOTE

As you can see, the Trengrouse clan is large and growing. That ball has a lot to answer for! The Trengrouse Ball stories can be read in any order, but they all have at least one scene set on the night of the ball. I've tried to avoid spoilers as much as possible from book to book, truly I have. The stories start and end on different days, overlapping in time. Some last a few days, others months. And characters move from one story to the other, so you will meet old friends, sometimes before they've met each other!

Characters with roles in this novella are in **bold**. Non-bolded characters may appear in other Trengrouse Ball books, or be referred to briefly in this story. More information on the novellas in brackets can be found after the last chapter.

This book is written and typeset in British/Australian spelling.

The Mandeville Household

Lady **Demelza Mandeville**, née Trengrouse
   John Mandeville, her husband, deceased
   Adelia and **Grace**, her twin daughters
   Sarah Lamb, their governess
   (See *The Lion and Miss Lamb*.)
   Mr and Mrs George Mandeville, the heirs apparent
   Servants:
   Mr Bushell, the butler
   Jonas, footman,
   Carter, lady's maid
   Mrs Griffiths, month-nurse

Nanny

The Kelynack Household

Sir Denzell Kelynack, baronet
Lady Kelynack, his mother

The Trengrouse Household
    Jory, Earl Trengrouse
    Maria, Countess Trengrouse, his wife
    Locryn, the eldest son and heir
    Ellestryn, Locryn's wife
    Petroc, son, Captain Trengrouse of His Majesty's Army (see *The Captain and the Lady*.)
    Endellion, son, importer/exporter (see *The Lion and Miss Lamb*.)
    Felix, son, mining engineer
    Melissa, daughter, twin to Ives
    Ives, son, landholder (see *The Youngest Son*.)
    Kate/Katie, his wife, née Kelynack, Denzell's sister (see *The Youngest Son*)
    Kerenza, daughter, youngest child (see

The Baboon at the Ball.)
    Servants:
    Mr Carveth, the butler
    Mrs Lovell, the cook
    Bryok, footman

Other Characters

Lady Beatrice Marlowe
    (See *The Captain and the Lady.*)
    Charles Goddard, Earl of Westholm
    Mr Gunson, a guest at Trengrouse Hall
    Mr Arasan, a guest at Mandeville House
(See *The Lion and Miss Lamb.*)

MORE FROM ELIZABETH LEYDIN

I hope you've enjoyed the third book in the Trengrouse Ball series. There are more—see below.

Sign up for Elizabeth's Substack blog, 'Corsets & Coaches', where she shares true-life Regency stories and tidbits, as well as news about her latest releases, or watch her "This Week in the Regency" videos on Youtube.

More Trengrouse Ball Sweet Regency Romances

The Trengrouse Ball books can all be read as stand-alones – the timelines overlap, but each story is separate.

The Captain and the Lady
Book 1 in the Trengrouse Ball series

Petroc Trengrouse has come home from Waterloo missing his right leg.

Family friend Lady Beatrice Marlowe has been thrown out of her home on the deaths of her father and brother.

When Petroc comes to stay at Beatrice's mother's seaside house to recover from his wounds, he has no idea that he's causing severe financial problems.

He feels he's not fit to marry; she knows she's too poor to attract an aristocratic suitor. Will the Trengrouse Ball prove both of them wrong?

The Youngest Son
Book 2 in the Trengrouse Ball series

When Ives Trengrouse hijacks his friend Den's coach after the Trengrouse Ball, he thinks it's no more than a prank. But Den isn't inside. Instead, it's his sister Katie, going home early with a migraine.

Compromised beyond saving, the two must marry immediately—and do so. Katie's dreams of a big London Season are gone. Ives can't go on his light-hearted, care-for-nothing way now he's a married man.

Neither of them wants to be in this marriage: can they turn childhood friendship into something deeper?

The Baboon at the Ball
Book 4 in the Trengrouse Ball series

A forbidden love story with animal antics to upset the normal order of things! (Or, a Cinderella story with a difference…)

Val Muffet is a Cit—a rich, well-educated, beautifully-mannered man, but definitely *not* one of the *ton,* despite being invited to the Trengrouse Ball.

Lady Kerenza Trengrouse's family is amongst the great and the good of the land, and she expects to marry a lord. An earl, at least!

What could bring these two to care about each other? Enter Genevieve, the lost, forlorn but definitely challenging baboon, given to the Muffets by the Prince Regent himself.

Genevieve is *not* invited to the ball, but she